Rigby

Letters/Faxes/E-mails

Written by Jill Eggleton

Illustrated by Trevor Pye

Michael Maloney's Mail

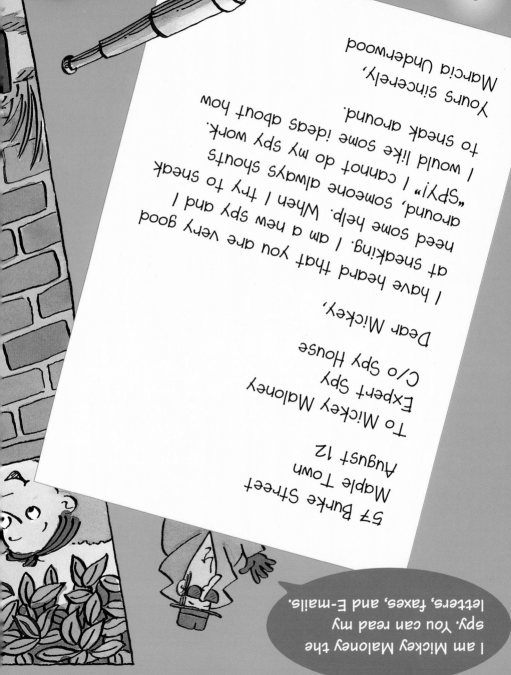

I am Mickey Maloney the spy. You can read my letters, faxes, and E-mails.

57 Burke Street
Maple Town
August 12

To Mickey Maloney
Expert Spy
C/o Spy House

Dear Mickey,

I have heard that you are very good at sneaking. I am a new spy and I need some help. When I try to sneak around, someone always shouts "SPY!" I cannot do my spy work. I would like some ideas about how to sneak around.

Yours sincerely,
Marcia Underwood

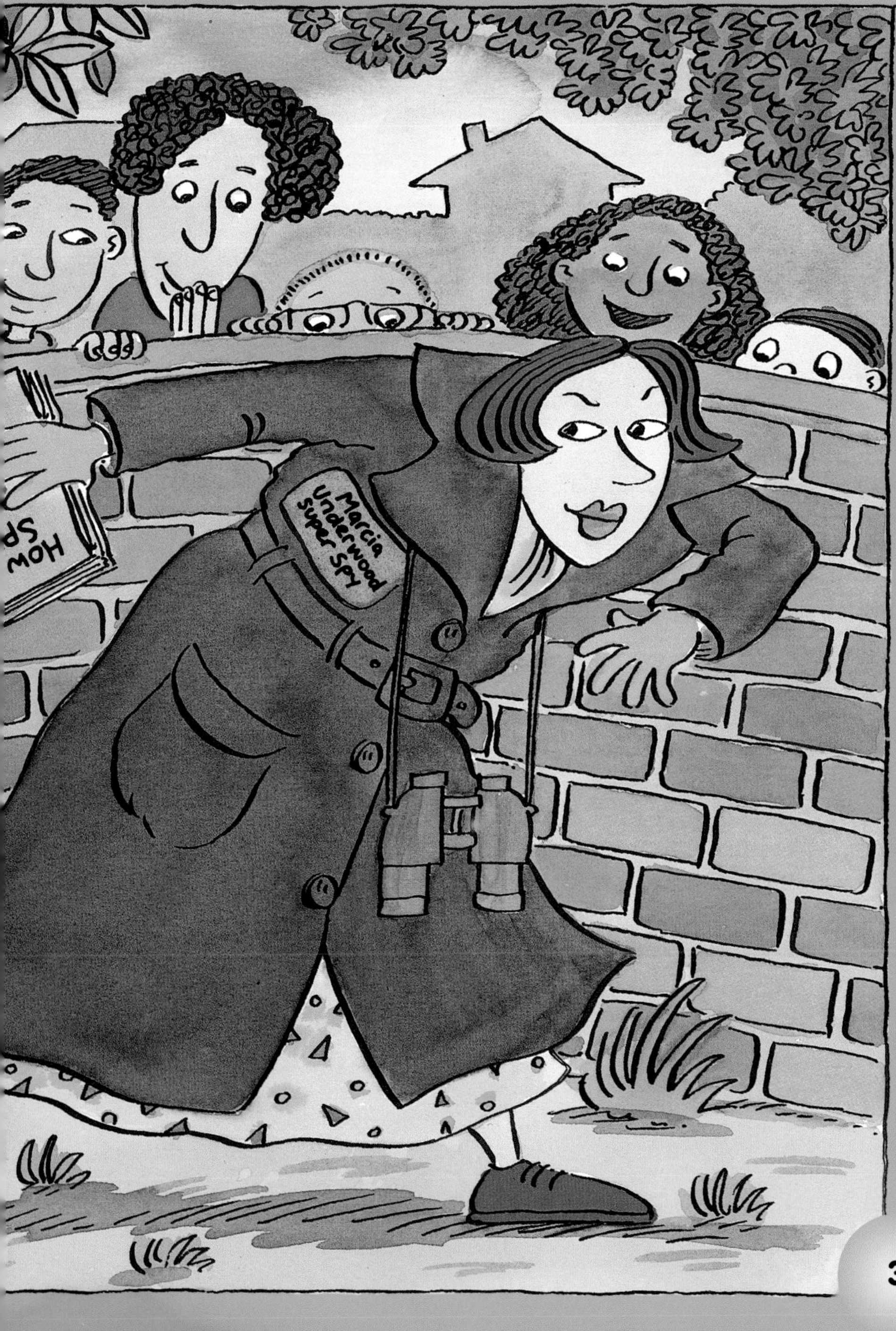
Marcia Underwood Super Spy

43 Tunnel Street
Boggyville
March 26

Dear Mickey,
How are you? I have been very
busy with lots of spy jobs.
Last week I had to find out why
the bird eggs were cracking.
I had to sit in a tree for two
days dressed like a leaf. I found
out the eggs were cracking
because the birds were sitting
on them!

I would like to hear all your
spy news, so write soon.

Love,
Maggie

E-mail from: bigwig@spilink.co
To: mickeymaloney@spilink.net
Sent: 2.45 am
Subject: Job

Re: Fluffy cat
Mr. Rick has a big, fluffy cat. Every night it comes home covered in sticky mud. Mr. Rick wants to know what it is doing and where it is going. You will need to follow this cat.

Be careful.

Big Wig

High Street
rraceville
ay 21

Mr. Maloney
71 Cook Street
Terraceville

Dear Mr. Maloney,

I am very pleased with the spying job you do. I know that you often have to get to places in a hurry, but please do not walk across people's gardens. The people in my town do not like footprints in their gardens.

Yours sincerely,
Des Nelson
Mayor of Terraceville

Fax to: Mickey Maloney
From: The Spy Shop
Date : 6/11

Re: Spy shoes and spy flashlight

We have the new spy shoes and the spy flashlight that you wanted. Please stop by to get them, as we cannot send them by mail.

Roy

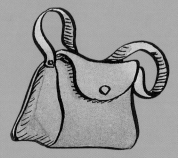

9

April 12th

Dear Mickey,
Thank you for finding out who was
making holes in my cabbages.
I didn't know I had so many snails.
You are a very good spy. I will call
you again when I need your help.

Rachel Terry

Invitation

To: Mickey Maloney
What: Spy Party
Where: Funkies
When: Saturday July 6
Time: 7.30pm
Dress: Casual orange clothes
Reply by: July 3

9 Brown Street
Terraceville
March 14

Dear Mr. Maloney,

I would like to say sorry for following you the other night. I did not know that you were a spy. I thought you were just sneaking around. I wanted to find out what you were doing.

I am sorry I frightened away the birds you were spying on. The next time I see you out on a job, I will know not to follow you.

Yours sincerely,
Matthew Gibson

15

Spy Ears and Eye Specialist

42 Nelson Street
Terraceville
August 14

To Mr. Maloney
71 Cook Street
Terraceville

Dear Mr. Maloney,

Your next visit to Dr. Simon is on Friday, August 30. Last time you had your ears looked at. This visit is to look at your eyes. Please tell us if you cannot come on Friday.

Yours sincerely,

Barbara Audrey
Secretary

Mail

Letters, faxes, and E-mails can:

Give information
Your appointment is on Friday, August 30.
Spy Party, Saturday, July 6

Ask questions
Could you give me some ideas about how to sneak around?

Apologize for something
I am sorry I climbed up the tree with you.

Thank someone
Thank you for finding out who was making holes in my garden.

Request something
I ask you not to take shortcuts . . .

Please stop by to pick up.

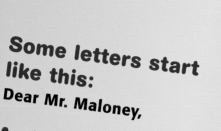

Some letters start like this:
Dear Mr. Maloney,

And end like this:
Yours sincerely,

Some letters start like this:
Dear Mickey,

And end like this:
Love,

Some letters or faxes or E-mails are friendly:
Dear Mickey,
How are you?

Some letters or faxes or E-mails are about business:
Dear Mr. Maloney,
Your next appointment with Dr. Simon is . . .

Guide Notes

Title: Mickey Maloney's Mail
Stage: Fluency (1)

Text Form: Letters, Faxes, E-mails
Approach: Guided Reading
Processes: Thinking Critically, Exploring Language, Processing Information
Written and Visual Focus: Sending Messages

THINKING CRITICALLY
(sample questions)
- What letter do you think is from a friend? How can you tell?
- Why do you think Big Wig sent Mickey Maloney an E-mail and not a letter?
- How else could the salesperson have told Mickey Maloney about the spy shoes?
- Which letter is asking for Mickey Maloney's help?
- What information does the letter from the doctor give Mickey Maloney?

EXPLORING LANGUAGE

Terminology
Spread, author and illustrator credits, ISBN number

Vocabulary
Clarify: invitation, casual, specialist
Nouns: mail, spy, garden, footprints, snails
Verbs: try, send, want, know
Singular/plural: job/jobs, footprint/footprints, hole/holes

Print Conventions
Apostrophes – possessives (Mickey Maloney's mail, bird's eggs, people's gardens),
    contraction (didn't)

Phonological Patterns
Focus on short and long vowel **o** (n**o**t, j**o**b, cl**o**thes, g**o**ing)
Discuss root words – making, getting
Look at suffix **ly** (sincere**ly**)